Magic & Wonder

Anthology 1:

Tales of Bards Aloud

By Gerry Donlon

SB

SOFTWOOD BOOKS

SUFFOLK, UK

Published and Manufactured by Softwood Books

EU Responsible person: Maddy Glenn
Office 2, Wharfside House, Prentice Road, Stowmarket, Suffolk, IP14 1RD
www.softwoodbooks.com, hello@softwoodbooks.com

EU Rep:
Authorised Rep Compliance Ltd., Ground Floor, 71 Lower Baggot Street,
Dublin, D02 P593, Ireland
www.arccompliance.com, info@arccompliance.com

A CIP catalogue record for this book is available from the British Library

Paperback ISBN: 978-1-0682596-0-9

Contents

The Deben River Sprite

Some people may have heard the legend of "The Groaning Stone of Debenham." It's said that the stone is resting at the bottom of the river Deben, at its source in the town of Debenham, Suffolk, and when the church clock strikes at midnight, the stone (allegedly) turns over and groans. But, not many people may know how the "groaning stone" got there …

Way back in time, many, many billions of years ago, a trickle of water rose from the ground near to what we now know as the town of Debenham. The water gradually made its way down a gentle slope and was joined by other trickles of water from here, there and everywhere. The "gentle" slope became steeper and steeper as those trickles and tributaries became a stream, and gradually after about three hundred and thirty-three million years that stream became a river, the River Deben.

The River Deben's water gained energy and created ripples as it flowed, making its way for many miles down by Woodbridge and Kyson Point, and then on it flowed by Martlesham Creek and terminated its journey into the sea at Felixstowe.

It was a night of a full moon when, where the river flowed by Woodbridge and down toward Kyson Point, a thunderstorm erupted and lightning struck the river in many areas, causing steam and mist to rise from the river. The ripples became more and more active, dashing back and forth from riverbank to riverbank. And when trillions of those ripples were washed up on the shore at Kyson Point, something magical happened. With Moon beams gleaming and thunder rumbling and lightning flashing, a tiny ripple went into labour and the beautiful Deben River Sprite was born from elemental forces!

The water sprite found a tiny cave on the riverbank, and she slept there until the sun rose the following morning. When she awoke, she stretched and yawned and then she made her way out of the cave into the daylight. She smiled and began to explore her beautiful new world. As she walked and skipped about, she noticed a very small stick and she picked it up to examine it, for she had never seen a stick before. There were a few little holes on a side of the stick, and on impulse she blew into some of them. It was amazing because there was a pleasant sound and as she placed her fingers on the tiny holes and blew into the top of the stick, beautiful music began to flow. That little stick was a magic flute, and its beautiful music floated up and down and right across the river to the other side, now known as Sutton Hoo. The music was heard by a demon, the Demon of the Deben. Well, the demon became enchanted by the music, and he crossed the river to see where it was coming from. He crept slowly up to Kyson Point and, when he peered around a gorse bush, he saw the beautiful sprite. He had never seen anything so beautiful in all his life, and he began to fall in love with her. The next day the demon went back and asked her to marry him. But the sprite said no, and that they could never be together or marry for he was born of a demon and she was born of water. The demon went back to his cave very unhappy, but the sprite continued to enjoy her happy and contented life.

Many years later, as a flock of starlings were making their way home to their reed beds near Kyson Point, they heard a sound so sweet that it stopped them in flight. It was the music from the magic flute of the river sprite. And they too were enchanted and mesmerised, for high in the sky they began to act strangely. They flew this way and that way, hither and thither, and that way and this way. They flew every way, but they never collided with each other. Eventually they were exhausted, and they dropped right down to the reed beds to sleep for the night. This was the very first murmuration ever performed, and you can still see murmurations of starlings at Kyson Point to this very day.

The demon of the Deben had been watching the starlings and, when he saw the magic the sprite could perform, he again wanted to marry her, but once again she said no and told him to get off home. The demon got very angry and frustrated and, as he walked home, he saw a large stone on the ground. In a temper, he kicked the stone. It rose off the ground and it flew right into the air, turning and turning and twisting and turning as it flew upstream from the force of the kick. The demon looked back at the sprite and shouted a curse on her. The demon said that the river sprite would lay dormant in her cave and the spell could not be broken until she heard a groan from a stone. The river sprite fell into a deep sleep in the tiny cave where she was born, and the beautiful music of her magic flute would not be heard again for millions of years …

But, while the Sprite lay dormant, other creatures were moving and evolving into various species, and one of those species became Humankind.

One day, hundreds and thousands of years later, some human beings began to find their way across Europe to Britain and Ireland, bringing their cultures and precious skills with them. Through time, populations grew and thrived, employment was created, and many historical monuments erected. Rich employers began casting bronze bells to wake and call their workers to the fields and other places of employment. One of those bells was erected by a landowner near Debenham at the beginning of the fifth century. The first time the bell was rung near Debenham to awaken the workers, it also awakened something else! It was the stone the demon of the Deben had kicked there all those millions of years ago when he put a spell on the Deben River Sprite! As the bell rang out, the stone turned over and groaned so loudly that the groans sent sound waves and ripples through the waters of the Deben, right down to Kyson Point and beyond.

And there in her tiny cave at Kyson Point, under a spell and asleep for many lifetimes, was the Deben River Sprite who had waited for this moment. For this was the moment that the spell was broken and she was awakened. And as time passed by, the beautiful sprite was back to her wondrous ways again.

In the middle of the fifth century, a jay who had buried and stored hundreds of acorns in a forest close by for the long harsh winter months ahead was now on a journey to uncover and eat his last one. As he flew over Kyson Point to the forest for his acorn, he looked down and saw something he had never seen before on this journey. It was the river sprite, and she was playing her beautiful, magic music. At first he thought she would make a tasty breakfast, but when he heard the music he felt very disorientated. He flew around in circles for some time and got dizzy, and then he flew far away in the opposite direction, therefore forgetting about his last acorn.

One day, about two hundred years later, a king and some of his warriors were sailing up the river Deben to Woodbridge. The king asked his warriors to stop. They stopped at what we now know as Sutton Hoo. He told his warriors to source an oak tree that, he said, must be strong and must be long. The warriors went into the forest close by and soon found an oak tree that was very strong and very long. The king said he was going to build a ship to be buried in, and this oak tree would make a fine keel for the ship. That king was called Rædwald, and if that jay bird had remembered where he had buried his acorn all those years ago, there may never have been a burial ship at Sutton Hoo.

So, the next time you're in the lovely town of Woodbridge, take a walk along the river path to Kyson Point, and if you happen to see a murmuration of starlings, listen out for the music of the Deben River Sprite, for she will surely be close by, still playing her magic flute.

When the Church bell strikes at midnight
near the dreamy Deben source,
a river stone awakens and turns over,
then groans with extreme force.
For this is where the river Deben
begins its outward journey flow,
streaming its way through a winding course,
on its way to Felixstowe.

Its headwaters begin trickling in Debenham,
or so the ancient story goes.
Then it cuts a course to Woodbridge,
gaining energy as it grows.
And as it winds its way round Kyson Point,
the rivers magic bursts into light.

For there, cavorting along the grassy banks,
you may see the Deben River Sprite.

She twirls and dances to the Deben's song
as its waters gush and rush on by.
Then she plays a tune on her magic flute
to the starlings as they flock on high.
A murmuration can soon be seen,
for the starlings are now bewitched in flight.
By the spirit and magic of the Deben
and the music of its delightful river sprite.

So, let us love our meandering river
and let us show it some respect.
For far too long and in recent times
it has been subjected to severe neglect.
Let's all nurture its life-giving waters
for those generations yet to delight
in its mystery and in the magic
of the Spirit of the Deben,
and its undine river Sprite.

The Flight of the Stag Beetles

Suffolk has a well-established population of stag beetles. Wedged between the Deben and Stour rivers their colonies appear to thrive. They sure are remarkable creatures: the female spends much of her time crawling on the ground, and many males fly upright buzzing with their wings flapping behind them like a faery. Females will lay their eggs in rotting wood underground and then their larvae will spend up to seven years just eating and eating and growing and growing. Many people have tried to determine why the males fly in such a peculiar manner. Some say it is to attract a mate, but I'm not too sure about that, so this is my theory.

When the Romans were establishing themselves in Britain in the second century CE, they rapidly expanded north. When they reached the area now known as Newcastle, on the east coast of England, they were getting unwelcome visitors coming from further north. Those unwelcome visitors would plunder and rob anything they could lay their hands on and come back for more. The Romans decided they would have to keep those undesirables at bay, so they started to build a wall across from Newcastle in the east to Bowness-on-Solway in the west. It was about one hundred and twenty kilometres long and about five meters high. It was built mostly of stone in the east and about three meters wide. Over in the west it was build mostly of turf and was up to six meters wide. This alone kept most of those unwelcome visitors out, but it also kept some welcome creatures from going about the valid business of their annual migration. Those welcome creatures were the wonderful stag beetles.

When the stag beetles realised they couldn't fly higher than the wall, they decided to construct a platform made of oak logs that would carry them up and over the wall. Days and weeks were occupied sourcing and gathering one hundred logs suitable for a long journey. Each and every log was connected together with tough nettle fibre string, tough pieces of animal hairs, and sheep's wool. The stag beetles plaited and wove the hair and wool with their "kneaded" antennae to give the strings more strength. Females then began to lay their eggs in some of the logs to take with them on the flight. Some of the males gathered lots of various herbs that the Romans had abandoned on the north side of the wall. They stashed the herbs between many cracks and in holes in the logs. This would be part of their sustenance on the journey and their first attempt at thyme travel! Just before they were ready for takeoff, three million, three hundred and thirty-three thousand, three hundred and thirty-three stag beetles reported for duty.

Approximately thirty-three thousand, three hundred and thirty-three were assigned to each of the one hundred logs. Once they had tied their hind legs to their logs with the remaining nettle fibre string they were ready for the off. Soon their wings began to flap, slowly and slowly at first, then faster and faster and faster! Then thirteen million, three hundred and thirty-three thousand, three hundred and thirty-two stag beetle wings began to power their powerful platform. Slowly but surely they lifted it from the ground to the sky. For hours their wings were beating, flapping, and fluttering, taking them higher and higher, until eventually they were clear of the unwanted wall.

A huge, unseasonable storm erupted, and a strong, cold north wind took those stag beetles and their platform many miles to the south. For weeks and months, they travelled like a huge dark cloud in the sky, clinging on to their precious cargo as best they could. But there was a price to pay. All their exertions from the flapping, fluttering, and beating of their wings, doing their utmost best and trying to hang on to those essential logs hanging from their hind legs, had taken its toll. As they arrived over Suffolk those wonderful stag beetles were extremely exhausted. The oak platform was getting lower and lower to the ground. Eventually, as they hovered over an ancient wood near Ipswich, most of the nettle fibre strings snapped, followed by the unravelling animal hair and wool. Sadly, many of the logs plummeted to the ground, taking their stag beetles with them. Some of the logs were embedded in the soft earth with their occupants still attached. The remainder of the logs fell at random, also getting embedded in the boggy surroundings.

Thousands of Stag Beetles had given their lives to secure a new life and habitat for their offspring. The following year, millions of the eggs that were laid in the logs hatched and the Stag Beetle cycle began all over again.

That is my theory of why stag beetles fly as they do - the weight of the oak log platform tied to their hind legs for months meant they couldn't straighten their legs afterwards, and they have been flying upright to this very day. And if you're ever walking in a meadow bordering on Spring Wood, the remnants of their platform is still visible and is now said to be the largest stag beetle pile in the world.

The Seven Pirates Who Became Invisible

For the biggest part of the 13th century, Dunwich, Suffolk, was a major port in East Anglia. Ships from there sailed to and from ports to countries far and wide. The town was thriving and trade with Europe was brisk. Some people came from all over Suffolk and East Anglia to find employment, and some more came for various other reasons. Then along came devastating storms in 1286 and 1287 that put a stop to the good times and brought about a steady decline. Piracy was particularly potent on the high seas during that era and was getting more popular. Many pirates became famous - for one reason or another - during that time.

This is a story about seven pirates who became famous for one particular reason, and that reason was, they became invisible. One fateful night, by sheer coincidence, seven strangers met in an inn in the town of Dunwich. It was less than a year before the first devastating storm of 1286.

All of them were very poor. All of them wore tattered and torn or patched clothes and boots. All of them had a gunny sack over their shoulder to carry their small supply of food and water in. They had arrived from seven different sections of Suffolk, and each and every one of the men had one desire in common. That desire was to become a pirate, for surely a pirate's life was an easy life: treasure was just fed up of being in peoples' drawers and not seeing the light of day and just pleading to be pirated. Once strong ale began taking effect, their tongues began wagging and their mouths began to run away with them. It so transpired that each and very one of them were there to steal a ship, to sail the high, the low and the seven seas, and to live a life of luxury thieving tons of tempting treasure. It also transpired, during the partaking of more strong ale, that, not one of them had a parrot, not one of them had an eye patch, not one of them had a peg leg, not one of them had a hook hand, not one of them could say "ARRRR me 'arty," not one of them sailed a ship before, not one of them had ever been on a ship before, not one of them had ever been to sea before, and not one of them could swim. And most importantly of all, not one of them had a drop of rum about their person. But hey, what could go wrong, they said, if they all joined forces and pooled their resources, their skills, and their talents together. So, the first thing they decided upon was to steal a ship, and of course they were in the right place for that. For just a short hop, skip, and a jump from the inn were hundreds of ships of all descriptions lined up, some in the harbour and some a little offshore. And as the church bells rang for midnight, they hopped, skipped, jumped, and staggered their way to the port and deduced that whilst the ships in the harbour would be full of food and water, they wanted an empty ship to carry their pirated treasure home, and of course, the offshore ships were closer to the seven seas too. So, a ship offshore it was going to be, but how were they to get out there? After a few slurred discussions one of them proposed stealing a small rowing boat, for had he not once seen, with his own two eyes, a sailor in a small boat rowing to a big ship and then tying the small boat to the big ship? The rest of them looked at each and said, "why didn't we think of that!" It was now dark but somehow, between them, they could see enough to steal a rowing boat and then row it offshore to where an empty ship awaited them. Well, they tied the little boat to the back of the ship and all managed to clamber aboard. They had a good look round and kind of acquainted themselves with their surroundings in the dark. Not knowing what to do, and thinking they knew everything, they started tugging at this rope and pulling at that rope until they all collapsed on the deck with exhaustion and were soon fast asleep. Not only were they a motley crew, but they looked to be a moth-eaten crew as well.

By some amazing good luck or great judgment, the ropes they had tugged and pulled were attached to the sails and the sails were now flying high. During the night, as the seven slept, a storm erupted, and those sails had begun straining at the seams and dragging the ship into open waters. As they began to wake up in the morning, reality struck. All they could see was water - oceans of water. Where were they, they asked, but no one knew the answer. One of them piped up and asked, "Who is the captain? The captain should know where we are." There was scratching of heads and loud mumblings, but no one knew. "Did we elect a captain?" mumbled someone, but no one could remember. "Right, let's elect a captain!" came a shout. But no one could agree on who to elect, so, in an ideal, democratic way, all seven were elected captain. And so it was, the next question that came from Captain 5 was, "What are we going to name our ship? Every successful pirate ship has a name."

There were more scratching of heads and loud mumblings before Captain 7 piped up, "How about the 'Seven Captains'?" the other six captains agreed straight away without any objections and the seven captains were now captains of the "Seven Captains." Sometimes life can be that simple.

Then Captain 1 asked "What are we having for breakfast? I'm hungry" all the captains searched all around the ship, looking in cupboards and drawers, but not one crumb did they find.

"Can I have a drink of water?" asked Captain 2, but there was no water either.

"Whose great idea was it to leave the ships that were full of food and water?" Captain 4 asked.

"It was the captain's great idea!" shouted the rest of the captains.

"But I have some food and water in my sack," said Captain 6.

"Where is your sack?" they all asked.

"I think I left it in the small boat last night," he answered.

"Well," said the rest of the captains, "mine must be there, too." They ran to the stern of the ship and nearly tripped over a huge anchor.

"What is that huge iron fishing hook for?" asked Captain 4.

"It must be to catch sharks and whales," answered Captain 6.

They looked down and saw the seven sacks scattered about in the boat. Captain 2 said, "Leave it to me, I'll go down and grab them." He got into the little boat, grabbed the sacks, and threw them up on to the deck. A hearty breakfast was eaten by all, washed down with water, but they knew their supply of food and water wouldn't last them very much longer.

The ship was now miles and miles out to sea and a big debate followed. Where were they going? Was there a map or a compass? Who was going to steer the ship? Another search of the ship was proposed. "Search every nook and cranny and bring everything you find to the deck," said Captain 7.

"Aye aye, captain," said the other six captains (they were beginning to learn pirate speak by now).

The search turned up a map, a ship's compass, and a very

long rope. All items were taken to the deck as requested. The map showed the way to the seven seas but only Captain 2 had a vague idea how to read the compass. At least a few of the captains had an idea how to read the map, and the rope might come in handy if they were to take prisoners while pirating. "Right, fellow captains," said Captain 3 as he looked at the map, "according to this map we could be in the seven seas and ready to pirate. To make quite sure, I want us all to spread out on the ship and have a good look. Captains 7, 1, and 6, you go up the top deck, climb the masts, and have a good look from there. Captain 4, you go to the front of the ship. Captain 2, you go to the back of the ship. And Captain 5, you go to the left side. I'll stay here on the right side. We will all meet back here in ten minutes and tell what we saw."

All the captains went to their positions and after ten minutes they were all back on deck. "From your vantage points, tell us what you saw," said Captain 3. "Captains 7, 1, and 6, what did you see?"

"I saw a sea," said captains 7, 1 and 6.

"Now, captains 2 and 4, from your vantage points what did you see?"

"I saw a sea," said captains 2 and 4.

"Now, captains 5 and 3, from your vantage points what did you see?"

"I saw a sea," said captains 5 and 3.

"Well, each of us has seen a sea, and, as there are seven of us, I conclude that is the seven seas we saw, which means we are in the seven seas and ready for some pirating!"

"HUZAAAAAH!" seven captains roared.

Well, they had got this far, and by now you may have guessed that, between them, they had become accustomed to lowering and hoisting the sails. Each captain had their own kind of skills. Although not many, the few skills they possessed had kept them afloat thus far. There were other little jobs too that they had kind of mastered, and they were now itching to go pirating.

Captain 7 saw a ship away in the distance, bobbing up and down on one of the seas. "Get them sails hoisted, captains, and follow that treasure; we're about to become paid pirates!" he roared, pointing to the distant ship. Well, all hands on deck got to do something or other, and before too long they were in pursuit of their first victim. The wind picked up and sent the ship skimming across the wavy sea, but they never got any closer to their victim. For the next seven days, seven different times, seven ships were chased by the Seven Captains, but with the same result, because those "victims" could see them coming seven nautical miles away and didn't hang about for confrontation. The crew of the Seven Captains was now depressed and hungry and thirsty. Their gunny sacks were empty. There was some meat left in the larder from six seasick seagulls that had crash-landed on deck the previous day, but they knew they had to consume that sparingly to make it last. Also, their last dregs of drinking water were nearly drained.

After realising the trouble they were in, Captain 1 called his fellow captains to a meeting on deck. "I'm afraid we are in dire straits-"

"How did we get there?" interrupted Captain 4. "When did we leave the seven seas?"

"Dire straits mean we are in deep trouble; we have no food or water, and no means of acquiring food or water," Captain 1 replied.

Seven faces became seven times longer once they all realised their dilemma. "I suggest we turn and sail for old Dunwich town. Some of us might just make it home alive," Captain 2 said. They all agreed, for they knew they had no choice.

Eventually they got the ship turned in the general direction they wanted, and off they sailed. Sometimes it's said that fortune favours the brave and this was one of those times. The wind was gentle and the Seven Captains had sailed only a short distance when Captain 5 shouted, "Over here! Over here!" The six other captains dashed across the deck and looked down to where Captain 5 was pointing. Bobbing about in the waves created by their ship, there appeared to be a large bottle. "It looks like it's full of water!" said Captain 5 excitedly, "that will keep our thirst quenched for days." Well, it sure did look like a large bottle of water, and the seven captains had to try and figure out how to seize it, because it was a long way down.

"I think we should all join together," Captain 3 suggested.

"What do you mean?" asked Captain 7.

"Well, if one captain leans over the deck and a second captain grabs his legs and lowers him down a bit, then a third captain grabs the second captain's legs and lowers those two captains down another bit, then a fourth captain grabs the third captain's legs and lowers those three captains down another bit, then a fifth captain grabs the fourth captain's legs and lowers those four captains down another bit, then a sixth captain grabs the fifth captain's legs and lowers those five captains down another bit, then the seventh captain grabs the sixth captain's legs and lowers those six captains down another bit, the captain nearest the water should be able to grab the bottle and hold on to it till we drag him back up on deck. But remember, every captain must hold on very tightly to their fellow captain's legs, because we don't want to lose that bottle or a captain."

For once, all the other captains understood Captain 5's logic. Now it came to choosing who would be first, etc., and surprisingly that didn't take too long either.

"Me first," said Captain 6.

"Me second," said Captain 3.

"Me third," said Captain 1.

"Me fourth," said Captain 5.

"Me fifth," said Captain 7.

"Me sixth," said Captain 4.

"And I'll be quite happy to dangle the lot of you over the edge," quipped Captain 2.

For once, everything went exactly to plan. Captain 6 leaned over the bulwark and Captain 3 grabbed him by the ankles and lowered him down until he himself was leaning over the bulwark. Now Captain 1 grabbed the ankles of Captain 3 and lowered him and Captain 6 down until he himself was leaning over the bulwark. Now Captain 5 grabbed the ankles of Captain 1 and lowered him, Captain 3, and Captain 6 down until he himself was leaning over the bulwark. Now Captain 7 grabbed the ankles of Captain 5 and lowered him, Captain 1, Captain 3, and Captain 6 down until he himself was leaning over the bulwark. Now Captain 4 grabbed the ankles of Captain 7 and lowered him, Captain 5, Captain 1, Captain 3, and Captain 6 down until he himself was leaning over the bulwark. Now Captain 2 grabbed the ankles of Captain 4 and lowered him, Captain 7, Captain 5, and Captain 1, Captain 3, and Captain 6 down until he himself was standing securely against the bulwark.

"Can you seize that bottle, Captain 6?" shouted Captain 2.

"I think so, if you could dangle me just an inch or two more," answered Captain 6. They huffed and they puffed and they pulled, until, eventually, they stretched a couple of inches and Captain 6 shouted, "GOTCHA!"

"Remember, captains, no 'HUZAAAAAH-ing' until every captain is safely back on deck!" shouted Captain 2.

Getting them all back on deck wasn't going to be easy, for they now had a big bottle of water to contend with and six captains hanging upside down with the blood rushing to their heads. As a matter of fact, it seemed nigh on impossible, because Captain 2 had no chance of hauling the six captains, plus a bottle of water back on deck. He simply wasn't strong enough, and his arms were well aching from his exertions so far. "Fellow captains, I fear we are in dire straits again," he announced. "My arms are tired and I wont be able to haul you all up together."

"Well haul us up one at a time, then!" shouted Captain 6.

"How can I do that when you're hanging off of each other?" said Captain 2.

"With a rope - the rope we found when we searched every nook and cranny!" shouted Captain 3.

"It's there on the deck beside you!" shouted Captain 1.

Captain 2 looked and, sure enough, the long rope was on deck by his feet. "Right," said Captain 2, "what I'm going to do is this: I'm going to let go of one of Captain 4's legs, then grab the rope. I'll then try and bind his leg to this rail I'm leaning on with my free hand. Then I'll let go his other leg and bind it to the rail with my two hands. I shall then tie my gunny sack to the other end of the rope and throw it down to Captain 6. When Captain 6 grabs the rope, he will put the water bottle into the gunny sack, and I'll haul it up on deck. Next, I will throw the rope to Captain 6 again, and this time he will secure the rope under his armpits and around his chest. When he's ready, I'll pull the slack from the rope and tell Captain 3 to release Captain 6's legs. Then I'll haul Captain 6 up and on to deck. Once he's safely on deck, we will repeat procedure with Captain 3, Captain 1, Captain 5, Captain 7, and Captain 4. Now, Captain 6, are you ready?"

"Aye aye, Captain 2!" he shouted.

Captain 2 carefully released his hold from one of Captain 4's legs. When he was happy that he could hold on with one hand, he reached down and picked the rope up with his free hand. He then wound the rope round Captain 4's ankles and secured it to the bulwark. He then released Captain 4's other leg and tied it to the bulwark. He then tied the rope around his gunny sack with both hands, drew in the loose rope, looked down and shouted, "Are you ready, Captain 6!"

"Yes I am, Captain 2!" shouted back Captain 6.

Captain 2 swung the rope and its attachment a few times then shouted, "Coming down!" He threw the rope down and surprisingly it landed right beside Captain 6, who was able to open the gunny sack with one hand and place the bottle inside.

"Haul away!" shouted Captain 6. Captain 2 hauled the gunny sack, with the bottle inside, up on deck and placed it in one of the many nooks and crannies on deck. He gathered the rope and swung it down again to Captain 6 who this time managed to do as Captain 2 had briefed earlier, securing the rope under his armpits and around his chest. "Haul away!" he shouted again. "I'm fed up hanging around here!"

Captain 2 gathered the slack and shouted, "Captain 3, prepare to release the legs of Captain 6!"

"Aye aye, captain, can't wait!" shouted Captain 3.

"Now!" roared Captain 2 and Captain 6 fell head first into the sea, then surfaced, also head first. Captain 2 was now taking the strain of the rope and hauling Captain 6 slowly up the side of the ship. Every time he hauled a little, he wound some rope around the rail to take the weight. It took some time, but the dripping head of Captain 6 eventually appeared above deck and Captain 2 pulled him on board from there. Next to be rescued was Captain 3, followed by Captain 1, followed by Captain 5, followed by Captain 7, followed by Captain 4. Amazingly, it all went without a hitch. As each captain was hauled aboard they helped out with hauling in the next one, until all captains were reunited on deck again. "Now we can 'HUZAAAAAH!'" said Captain 2, and seven "HUZAAAAAHs!" erupted from the Seven Captains ship.

"Where is the bottle of water?" asked Captain 7.

"Oh, sorry," said Captain 2, "it's in that nook over there. Let's all have a drink"

"I suggest that Captain 5 has the first drink because he saw the bottle in the water," said Captain 1.

Everyone agreed, including Captain 5. Captain 7 handed the bottle to Captain 5, who clamped his few teeth on the wooden stopper and twisted it this way and that way. He then pulled as it twisted until the stopper came out. He took a good swig and gave the bottle to Captain 2. While Captain 2 was having a swig, Captain 5's head was vanishing! Then the rest of his body vanished! "What's happened to Captain 5?" exclaimed Captain 3. "He's gone!"

"But I am still here," said a voice coming from where Captain 5 had stood. "I can see you all."

By now Captain 2 had had his swig and handed the bottle to Captain 6. "Ah, there you are, Captain 5," said Captain 2, who had also vanished.

"It looks like they can still see each other although we can't see them, so I'm taking a good swig as well," said Captain 6.

"Me too," said Captain 4 as he grabbed the bottle from Captain 6, who also vanished.

"I'm next," said Captain 1, taking the bottle from Captain 4 just before he vanished. Captain 1 took his swig and passed the bottle to Captain 7 who took his swig before passing the bottle to Captain 3 who took his big swig. Now all seven pirates appeared to be invisible, but they could all see and talk to each other! Captain 3 splashed a little of the contents on the small boat, and yet there was plenty more left in the bottle if ever needed for "emergency repairs." And although they were still hungry, their thirst was well and truly quenched.

As they had spent so much time trying to retrieve the water bottle and swigging from it, they hadn't noticed a storm moving swiftly towards them. Huge waves were being pushed in their direction by a loud, thunderous wind and torrential rain. The seven captains began to panic; being invisible didn't make them immune to the forces of nature. They made their way to hide in some of the nooks and crannies and hoped to last the storm out. No one had mentioned anything about storms at sea and the damage they can do. Waves upon waves were lashing over the deck from stern to helm, from port side to starboard side, and everywhere else in between. The seven captains clung to whatever they could, in their sanctuaries, to try and not be washed overboard. The Seven Captains ship, although getting tossed about relentlessly, seemed to like all the fuss as it rode every wave that was forced on it. One massive wave came at them and forced the helm so high that the ship almost doubled over backwards. That forced all the water down to the stern, taking the invaluable water bottle from its nook. The ship overcame that wave too, and, as the helm nosedived, the water was forced from the stern back to the helm, taking with it the invaluable water bottle along the deck. The rain suddenly stopped, the storm eased, but the sea was still choppy, and the deck was almost drained of its excess water. The seven now-invisible captains emerged slowly from their nooks and crannies to stand on the deck and look for any damage. As they stood there, looking, the ship's helm rose again on a rogue wave. The invaluable bottle went skidding from side to side along the damp deck to the stern and smashed against the huge iron fishing hook, spilling its contents. Some of the contents escaped through a small hole in the stern and dripped down onto the little boat below. "Oh no!" cried Captain 1, "Our reserves are gone!" Just then, the ship nosedived and the spillage from the bottle began a slow, slippery journey from the stern to the helm. The seven invisible captains, still standing on deck, watched with their mouths wide open as the contents of the bottle made its slow, slippery journey. For in its wake, the stern, the anchor, the deck, and everything else was disappearing! Now there were seven invisible captains standing on an invisible ship!

"This is great news indeed," said a smiling Captain 3.

"Why's that then, Captain 3?" asked Captain 5.

"Well, fellow captains, it means that with an invisible ship we can now sneak up on our victims without being seen and pirate away all day!"

"HUZAAAAAH! HUZAAAAAH!" roared the six fellow pirates.

"Does that mean if the ship is invisible, the wind and rain can't see it and we'll stay dry and storm free?" enquired Captain 2. No one answered, because no one knew. They all slept well that night knowing that no sea monsters or ghost ships could see them. The following morning, when they woke up, the sea was relatively calm and so were they. They set about sharing the last of the six seasick seagulls' meat and any other remnants they could shake out of their gunny sacks. Just after they had finished, Captain 1 pointed to the horizon and said, "I do believe that is a ship over there." All the captains eyed the horizon and, sure enough, there was a ship, and it seemed to be getting bigger and bigger.

"It's coming this way!" exclaimed Captain 2. "We have a victim; prepare to pirate!" The victim ship got closer and closer until it was nearly alongside the Seven Captains. They could see many people eating and drinking, music was playing, there was singing and dancing, and they could hear talking and laughing. There were dukes and earls and lords and ladies and other gentry on board.

"Now we need three captains to remain on board our ship and keep abreast of the victim so the four other captains can go pirating," said Captain 7. Captains 5, 2, and 6 volunteered to stay. "As each captain returns with treasure, one of you can replace him and join in the pirating," Captain 7 said.

"What about food and drink?" asked Captain 6.

"Ah, good thinking, Captain 6. Every captain going to pirate must take their gunny sacks and stuff them with treasure, food, and drink," replied Captain 7. And with that, the four captains who were pirating first boarded the ship, unseen and unheard. Those four captains were having a whale of a time. They sat at dining tables and ate the finest food, drank the finest ale, beer, and mead. When they had had their fill, they stuffed their gunny sacks with what remained and then went on a treasure hunt. Undetected they entered cabins of the rich and famous, and pirated the finest jewellery. It was not long before they returned to their own ship, loaded with lovely loot.

"Now, captains 5, 2, and 6, it's your turn and don't get caught!" laughed Captain 4 as he emptied his gunny sack and pockets of treasure, food and wine. Captains 1, 7, and 3 did the same and then handed their gunny sacks to captains 5, 2, and 6, saying, "Fill them high, captains, fill them high!" The last three captains boarded the treasure ship and continued where the first four captains had left off. They, too, stuffed their bellies and gunny sacks. They, too, wandered in and out of cabins, pirating fine jewellery until they could carry no more. The four captains helped them back on to their ship and also helped them empty their sacks and pockets, and then they pooled all their resources. Not only were they now seven bona fide pirates, they were seven bona fide invisible pirates!

The food and drink they'd pirated would last them for weeks, and the jewellery probably a lifetime. As they were about to have their afternoon snooze they heard a commotion aboard the victims' ship. The music had stopped, the singing and laughing had stopped, all to be replaced with screams and shouts. "Who has stolen my diamond bracelet?" screamed one woman. "Who has stolen my ruby necklace?" screamed another. "Who has stolen my gold cufflinks?" one man raged,

"Who has been rummaging in my drawers? someone pinched my vanity box!" nother woman declared. There was chaos and confusion aboard the victim ship, but there was laughter and merriment aboard the invisible ship.

Well the seven captains had never been happier and never so well fed in their lives. Every other day another victim ship or two would appear and the invisible Seven Captains would sneak up on them. The seven invisible pirate captains would do what they had done to their first victim, and thus pirating continued on the seven seas. Days turned to weeks, weeks rolled into months, and months into seven years. By now, the Seven Captains was stacked with treasure, food, and alcohol from bottom to top. It could barely sail with the weight of its valuable cargo plus the weight of the seven captains who were still having a whale of a time. But all good things must come to an end, for the seven captains realised that they couldn't add anything else, valuable or not, to their cargo. They decided that it would be best to call a temporary truce to pirating and to just eat and drink as much as they could for weeks to help get the weight on their ship down. The more they ate and drank, the more space would be left for more treasure, they said.

A few days after their bountiful binge began, Captain 7 was on deck near the stern, upchucking over the bulwark. Watching where the contents of his last binge landed in the salty sea, he spotted an object. It was bobbing about and similar to the water bottle Captain 5 had found. He shouted to his fellow captains as he pointed into the sea "More water! More water!" The six captains made their way slowly to Captain 7 and looked at what he was pointing at.

"Oh, that could save us from being seen again. Let's all join together like we did last time" said Captain 4.

"Well I was left hanging around for too long the last time," said Captain 6, "so this time I suggest we should get in the small boat, lean over the edge a bit, and pick the bottle up that way."

The six other captains stood there staring at Captain 6 and then shouted, "Why didn't we think of that? why didn't you think of that the last time?" After a short discussion it was decided that captains 6, 3, and 1 would stay on board and the other four would get in the small boat and rescue the bottle. This was much simpler than the first rescue and the whole operation took less time to do right than it took to explain how they did it wrong the first time. Captains 5, 7, 4, and 2 got back on board carrying the bottle, but this bottle was much smaller than the first one. The seven of them gathered round, each one inspecting the bottle in turn.

"We must not let this one get broken unless it's necessary," Captain 6 said.

"I say Captain 5 should open it; he was lucky the last time," said Captain 7, and all were in agreement. Captain 5 took the bottle and, as he had done before, clamped his teeth on the wooden stopper and followed the same procedure until the stopper came out. They all looked and waited.

"What is in it?" asked Captain 4.

"Well there's no water; it seems to be empty," replied Captain 5.

"Give me a look," said Captain 6, and he took the bottle for a closer inspection. He held it up to the light, turning it slowly as he tried to look down the neck and through the glass which obscured the contents. He said, "It is dry, but it looks like there is something inside circling the bottle, and the only way to see what it is is to break the bottle."

There were mumblings among the captains, then Captain 2 said, "As there is no magic water in it, we might as well have a smashing time!"

They all roared "HA! HA! HA! HE! HE! HE!"

The seven captains gathered by the anchor and Captain 7 was invited to do the honours. He held the bottle by the neck and began to tap the bottle gently on the iron anchor, then harder and harder, until the bottle broke into smithereens, leaving a circular piece of paper. Captain 7 slowly and carefully unfolded the paper and after he had looked at it for a moment, said, "I think this is for you, Captain 3; you can read maps."

Captain 3 took the paper and studied it at length before saying excitedly, "Fellow captains, this is every pirate's dream; this is great news indeed! This is a treasure map and, if we follow it, we are likely in for more treasure, and a pirate can never have too much treasure! HUZAAAAAH!"

"HUZAAAAAH!" roared all the seven, invisible pirate captains.

"Tomorrow at first light our next voyage begins!" Captain 3 said.

"Where are we going? Where is the treasure?" asked Captain 1.

"I don't know for sure," replied Captain 3, "but let me show you the map. You see here, it says, with a circle around it and an arrow pointing, 'Seven Seas, you is here,' and arrows pointing away to another circle that says 'Treasure is here.' Well, we is here in the seven seas, so all we need to do is follow those arrows with the help of our map and compass readers." It all sounded quite simple, for had they not found their way here with the same logic?

At first light the seven invisible captains went to their now familiar workstations. The lineup was: Captains 5, 1, and 7 were sail hoisters and sail reefers. Captain 2 was helmsman and compass reader. Captain 3 was map reader and general miscellaneous. Captains 4 and 6 were gofers and general dogsbodies.

"Are you ready?" asked Captain 2.

"We were born ready!" shouted the six other captains.

"Then hoist the sails, captains 5, 1, and 7!" Captain 2 shouted.

The sails were hoisted and Captain 3 shouted, "Twiddle and turn the helm wheel and follow those arrows, Captain 2!" Captain 2 twiddled and fiddled, and the Seven Captains moved steadily on, following the direction of the arrows.

Because of the treasure overload, progress was slow, but progress was made despite their lack of maritime knowledge. And, of course, they and their ship were still invisible. With shouts here and shouts there, tempers ebbing and flowing, and the introduction of a few new swear words, the Seven Captains, after many weeks, had exited the seven seas. Somehow, they found themselves somewhere in the middle of the Sea of Darkness. "Are we there yet?" asked Captain 4.

"Where are we now?" asked Captain 6.

"What does the map show?" asked Captain 5.

"The map only shows arrows on the water pointing to where treasure is," replied Captain 3.

"What does the compass show?" Captain 5 asked.

"The compass shows that we should sail to where the sun comes up," said Captain 2.

"Twiddle and turn that wheel, then, Captain 2, and make haste for the sun!" said Captain 3.

With the wind blowing in the right direction, and sheer good luck, much haste was made. After three more days they had reached the British sea and that took them into the Germanic sea. "Twiddle left, Captain 2, twiddle left; it's up here somewhere!" shouted Captain 3 as he scanned the map.

It may seem highly improbable, but the seven invisible pirate captains were now on the last leg of their treasure hunt.

Sailing north in favourable conditions they soon saw the Kent coast. The following day they saw the Essex coast, and before sunset that day they were hugging the Suffolk coast. They were only a few hours from where they set out seven years previously, but they didn't know that. "I suggest we lower the sails and have an early night," said Captain 5.

"I agree," replied Captain 4, "then we'll scour this strange land in daylight." No one argued, for they were all in need of a good night's sleep, so they lowered the sails and went to their crannies to sleep, as they had done most nights since they went to sea, and never once had they thought of dropping the anchor to moor.

When they rose in the morning and had gorged more food, Captain 3 said, "Something peculiar has occurred overnight: according to the arrows on this map we are in sniffing distance of the treasure! HUZAAAAAH!"

"HUZAAAAAH!" roared all the seven invisible pirate captains. What they hadn't realised was that, like most nights, without anchoring, the ship could drift about for miles, and it usually did.

"But where is the treasure?" asked Captain 1.

"Right over there!" said Captain 3, pointing to the shore about half a mile away where there were ships of all sizes and descriptions, but not nearly as many as there was on the night they left.

They all looked in amazement and Captain 7 remarked, "Over there? Over there, you say? Sure is that not the harbour where we stole this ship seven years ago?"

"It looks very much different and further away," said Captain 5.

"Well, I can hear that church bell ringing, so this must be the right place," said Captain 1, and they all agreed. They were astonished for they couldn't believe their good fortune. Seven years at sea and coming home to more treasure!

"Let's get this ship as close as we can, then we'll all jump in the boat," said Captain 2, "and don't forget your gunny sacks; there's more treasure to be had!" They got within half a mile then all climbed in the boat and rowed the rest of the way to shore.

When they were all standing on the sandy beach, Captain 3 said, "Now, fellow captains, this map shows we are in the right place. We must take seven steps north. Have you got your compass at the ready, Captain 2?"

"Yes, Captain 3," came the reply. Captain 2 set his compass. "Follow me"

They followed Captain 2 for seven steps north. "Now, we must take seven steps east," said Captain 3.

Captain 2 set his compass again and said "Follow me."

They followed Captain 2 for seven steps east. "Now, we must take seven steps south," said Captain 3.

Captain 2 set his compass again and said, "Follow me."

They followed Captain 2 for seven steps south. "Now, we must take seven steps west," said Captain 3.

Captain 2 set his compass again and said, "Follow me."

They followed Captain 2 for seven steps west. And would you believe it, they ended up standing on the exact spot from where they started! Captain 3 said, "We dig here!" Then he scraped a cross in the sand with the heel of his boot.

"Who has a shovel?" enquired Captain 5. They all looked at each other saying "Oh, I never thought of that!"

They looked around and Captain 6 spotted a shovel stuck in the sand close by. He brought it back, held it out, and asked, "Who wants to do the honours?" Captain 4 put his gunny sack down, took the shovel from him, and began digging.

The other six invisible pirates formed a circle around Captain 4 and roared, "DIG! DIG! DIG!" It didn't take him long to dig and shovel the sand aside. When he was down to about twelve inches there was a thud on wood! He began to gently scrape the sand from the wood and exposed a lid. Great excitement was brewing among them all, for this was the buried treasure chest they had always dreamed of finding. "Lift the lid! Lift the lid!" came the cry. Captain 4 eased the blade of the shovel under the lid and started to prise it open - S-Q-U-E-EEEEK! The lid opened slightly, he then went to the other side and did the same again with the shovel - S-Q-U-E-EEEEK! He prised and prised and suddenly the lid was loose and easy to lift off.

"Show us what you've got, Captain 4!" said Captain 7. The circle had grown much smaller as every invisible pirate captain, with gunny sack on shoulder, gathered close in to see the buried treasure. Captain 4 slowly lifted the lid off the wooden chest and put it aside so he and his fellow pirates could look down on the treasure. But there were no gold or jewels in the chest, just a folded piece of paper.

"It must be another treasure map," said Captain 3, "let me take a look." Captain 4 gave him the piece of paper and they all watched in anticipation as Captain 3 unfolded the paper and started to read. "If you are reading this, you must be a pirate," he read. "I too was a pirate until I found buried treasure in this wooden chest, then I renounced pirating because it's not an easy life. I got cold and wet and seasick on the seven seas and beyond. Now, thanks to this treasure I found, I'm married and settled down with a lovely wife and lots of money. You, too, should do the same - it's easy to do. All you have to do is say out loud three times, 'I renounce pirating! I renounce pirating! I renounce pirating!'"

Well, that came as a bit of a shock; they hadn't seen that coming. Seven invisible pirate captains were standing there with seven very visible open mouths, looking down on an empty treasure chest they had sailed thousands of miles to find. "Ah well," said Captain 5, "sure we have more than enough treasure over there in our ship. I like the idea of settling down with a wife to treasure. I think I might renounce pirating."

The other captains looked at him, then Captain 1 said, "Well, it sounds cosy to me. What say the rest of ye?"

The rest of them mumbled and fidgeted for a few moments, then said, "Aye, it does sound cosy, and with our ship full of treasure, none of us will want for money or go hungry or thirsty again."

They were all in favour and once more formed a circle. Invisible Captain 4 renounced first, saying, "I renounce pirating! I renounce pirating! I renounce pirating!" He was followed by the rest of them renouncing three times as well. A shout came from over by the shore. "Hey, you scruffy lot of ruffians, why are you digging holes on the beach? You're too old for making sand castles!" An officer was making his way over to confront the seven pirates, who, unfortunately, were no longer invisible.

"What's happened to us, everyone can see us now!" said Captain 3. "Let's run to the boat and get back to the ship!"

They ran to the boat but could no longer see their boat. They looked to the ship but could no longer see the ship. "We must find somewhere to hide," said Captain 7, and they found themselves crawling under an upturned boat on the beach. "I think what has happened is this," said Captain 2. "We just renounced pirating, which means we are now not pirates. And, because we were invisible pirates, we can't be invisible now because we are no longer pirates, and we can't be pirates again because we renounced pirating three times. Are you following me?"

"Yes" they all answered.

"Does that mean, then, that you need to be invisible to see an invisible boat and an invisible ship?" asked Captain 3.

"Yes," they all answered.

"Which means unless we become invisible again we will never get our treasure because the ship remains invisible and we can't find it?"

"Yes," they all said.

"Does it mean that we are no longer captains?" asked Captain 6.

"No," said Captain 2. "Whatever happens, we will always be captains."

That lifted their spirits and brought a welcome smile to all their faces, though, for fear of been detected, they refrained from shouting

"HUZAAAAAH!"

Cramped beneath the upturned boat, Captain 1 said, "Is the coast clear, yet? we need to get out of here, I'm hungry and thirsty."

"But now we have no money to buy food or drink; it's all over there on a ship we can't see," replied Captain 5.

"When I was younger," said Captain 4, "I knew of an inn somewhere not far from here where we could steal some food. But I can't remember exactly where it was. We just go in, a few of us causes a disturbance, and when the innkeeper's attention is averted, the rest of us stuff our gunny sacks and scarper."

"A good idea," said Captain 5, as he peered out from under the boat. "The coast is clear," he said, "now let's go get a bite and quench our thirst."

They all crawled out from under the upturned boat and looked around, but Captain 4 didn't know which direction to walk. Captain 3 said, "My map doesn't show arrows to an inn, but maybe Captain 2 can find the way with his compass. Captain 2, is your compass at the ready?"

"It's in my gunny sack somewhere, Captain 3. I'll find it," replied Captain 2. He unfastened his gunny sack and began to search for the compass, and within seconds he roared, "WOW! WOW! GUESS WHAT I FOUND!"

"Your compass, I hope," replied Captain 3. "Now let's get on and steal some food and ale, I'm starving," he said.

Captain 2, with a grin as wide as the Suffolk sky - and clutching his gunny sack, walked up to each captain and said, "Take a look, captain! Take a good long look! Hunger or thirst will never darken our doors again!"

As each captain peered inside the gunny sack, looks of astonishment covered their faces, followed by, "Why didn't I think of that?" as they proceeded to unfasten their own. And sure enough, within each of their gunny sacks, was ample treasure! Treasure they had forgotten about, for they had had other things on their minds since they came ashore and made their "appearance." The excitement continued and a huge group hug followed.

"I would like to say how proud I am to have sailed and pirated the seven seas with you all," said Captain 3. "We seven pirate captains were a formidable force on the Seven Captains ship, before and after we became invisible. We stuck together through hard times and easy times, through hunger times and thirst times, and, thankfully, we will never have to eat a seasick seagull ever again!"

Seven roars of "HUZAAAAAHH!" rang out across Dunwich beach.

But don't forget, out there on some sea somewhere, is the invisible Seven Captains ship, full of treasure and just waiting to be seen …

The Toad Queen

If you ever find yourself near a little lane in south-west Ipswich, about two hours after sundown or about an hour and a half before sunrise, from the middle of February to the middle of April, you will be forgiven if you think there is something weird and odd going on there! This is the time of Toad Patrol, when a number of dedicated volunteers, with the welfare of our toads at heart, get together with buckets, high-vis jackets, clipboards, head torches, hand torches, and suitable clothing for all weathers, patrol up and down the lane. They pick up any toads, frogs, or newts and put them gently into buckets. Then their cargo is escorted across the lane and released close to their breeding ponds, away from the danger of deadly wheels of motor vehicles.

All the equipment needed is stored in a big wheelie bin, with its lid chained down, located inside an allotment gate about a half mile from the lane entrance. The keys to the allotment gate and the wheelie bin chain are usually in the safe keeping of "The Toad Leader." This is a person - man or woman - appointed to distribute the essential equipment to his or her patrollers and to watch out for any signs of danger. They could encounter speeding cars, abusive drivers, etc., as they patrol up and down the half mile lane, as many as six times a night or in the early morning.

To one side of the allotment gate is a small car park where some motorists go either when the sun goes down or before it rises. There can be weird carryings on spotted in some of the vehicles parked there by the keen eye of an alert Toad Leader and very bright torch, but those stories are for an older audience another time!

To the right of the allotment gate is another gate that leads to Millennium Wood. One evening when I was the Toad Leader a large crowd of us were on our way to collect our high-vis jackets, torches, clipboards, head torches, and buckets from the wheelie bin. We noticed the gate to the wood was open. I was the volunteer warden of the wood and I knew that gate should be locked at that time of the evening. I walked up the slope, pulled the gate to, and snapped the lock back on in position. As I returned down the slope, Sally, a young girl patroller, pointed out that there were huge hoof prints on the ground and they were leading through the gate into the wood, but there were no signs of any hoof prints returning. I thought, "well, no one should be horse riding through the Wood this time of the evening, so we may as well leave them to find their own way out."

We loved it when Sally joined us on patrol with her mum. She was about nine years old and very eager to save any form of wildlife. Sally also had an amazingly keen eye for spotting newts for us, as they are so small and can be very difficult to see on a dark, damp road surface. Hardly a patrol night would go by without us hearing her excited cry of "I've found one, and there's another one!"

This night, we collected all our patrol equipment and, as the last rays of the evening sun descended behind the ancient wood, we set about walking slowly up and down the lane. Every so often there was a shout of "there's one!" or "over here!" and then the toads, newts, or frogs would be picked up and placed gently into buckets. We had learned from amphibian experts to place males and females in separate buckets for their journey to the breeding ponds.

We did rather well that evening as weather conditions were favourable.

Toads like it to be about ten degrees Celsius with damp conditions when they are moving, and they are reluctant to move if it is less than six degrees.

We picked up about thirty-three toads, mostly male, but also three fine, fit females, three frogs, and another two newts, thanks to Sally.

After four "sweeps" up and down the lane we decided that was it for the evening. It was getting colder and there was little chance of further movement of amphibians that night. We made our way back down the lane to the allotment, where we put all our patrol gear back in the big wheelie bin.

The gate to the allotment where the wheelie bin is located is made of a steel frame with a mesh wire covering. When we returned to the gate, our torch light would shine through and enable us to see the bin. When we returned this night, we knew something was amiss: no matter how many torches were shone at the gate, not one ray of light penetrated to the bin or the allotment! It was pitch black, but the light was reflecting back on us! Then we heard a snort and saw a huge head, a head as big as, and blacker than, the wheelie bin. It was bobbing up and down, snorting - it was a horse's head!

As fear gripped me, I gripped the shoulders of brave Sally and eased her to the front of me. I peered over her shoulder to where the darkness and the horse's head were. Then we heard a voice, a high-pitched sort of squeaky voice, and it said, "We have been expecting you!"

As Toad leader I knew I had to take control of the situation, so, still peeping over brave Sally's shoulder, I stammered, "Who have you been expecting?"

The squeaky reply came back, "All of you! We have been expecting all of you … Come closer!"

With my teeth chattering and my knees knocking I reluctantly eased Sally further to the fore and I walked hesitantly behind her. We came to a halt beside the frame of a huge black horse! I said,

"You have a very squeaky voice for a huge black horse."

A reply came, saying "I am up here!" As one, we all automatically shone our torches to where the voice had come from, and there, sitting in the middle of the horse's back, looking down on us, was … a female toad!

"You are a female toad!" I gasped.

"Not just any old female toad," came the squeaky reply. "I am the toad queen"

"The toad queen? But what are you doing sitting on the back of a horse?" I enquired.

"As I said, waiting for you!" came the curt reply. Then her voice mellowed, and she continued. "The horse I am sitting upon is big, black Bob of Bobbits Lane. He is a true and reliable friend to all toad queens. Many, many eons ago, before the onset of man in these parts, my ancestor toad queen was making her way to the wet land and breeding ponds. It was about a three day hop from her colony in the wood. She was laden with eggs and had left in plenty of time for the journey. When she exited the wood to a boggy meadow, she found her path blocked by a huge object. It was too high to hop or crawl over, and so she decided to go along the side of the meadow until she was free of the obstacle. Eventually she came to what she thought was the end of the obstruction. But what she saw would change toad history forever, for what she saw was a huge head, unmoving and barely breathing. Looking closely, she could see it was a huge horse. It was very badly injured and not far from death. How long it had lain there in those soggy conditions she did not know. It appeared to be not much more than skin and bone, because it had not eaten for days, or maybe weeks.

"The toad queen inspected the horse, looking for signs of injury, until eventually she spotted something inserted in the frog of one hoof. After closer inspection, she could see it was a piece of flint. The surrounding area of the wound was covered in yellowish pus, and the fetlock was swollen and infected. Forgetting about her migration to the breeding pond, the toad queen, for three days and three nights, set about nibbling away at the infected area. She broke away shards of flint and nibbled away at the pus-infected skin, until at last the shards became loose and she was able to dislodge them with force from her hind legs. She still continued to clean the open wound and infected area by nibbling and licking until all signs of the infection had disappeared. She then made a short journey and gathered some pieces of sphagnum moss and a dock leaf, for she knew they had healing properties. She chewed and chewed the dock leaf until it was a mush, then mixed it with the spongy sphagnum moss. She then gently pressed some of the mixture into the open wound and rubbed the remainder around the fetlock. By now she was very tired and soon she fell asleep. The following morning, when she awoke, the horse began to twitch and move. There was long grass close to his head, and he set about eating it. He moved his head hither and thither, eating all the grass within his range, and then fell asleep with exhaustion. The toad queen stayed by his side, watching over him, sometimes wiping beads of rolling sweat from his brow and long face. After another sunrise the horse awoke and looked around. He swished his tail and he tried to get to his feet. After hours of trying, he managed to get on his front knees and, soon afterwards, he was standing on all fours, wavering and tottering, but he did not fall down, and was able to continue eating more grass that he was now able to reach.

When he had eaten his fill and was steady and rigid on his feet, Bob looked at the toad queen, bowed his head close to her, and said, "Thank you for saving my life, your Majesty. Is there anything I can I do for you?"

"I am weary now," she said, "time is running out for me to reach the breeding ponds. Would you carry me there, please?" The horse picked her up in his mouth and placed her on his back and walked her to the breeding ponds, where he lowered her down by the edge near a clump of grass. There were not many toads left at the pond, as most of them had been and gone. The horse could see she was not well after all her exertions and watched as she feebly entered the water. Soon there was a male toad on her back and clinging to her shoulders. Bob watched as she dispersed her eggs close to some reeds and the male toad fertilised them. To his dismay, Bob then saw her sink to the bottom of the pond. He moved closer and dipped his head deep into the murky water and grabbed the toad queen in his mouth. Big black Bob took her to an open piece of ground where he opened his mouth and gently laid her on a soft clump of moss, but it was too late. He could see that the toad queen, that beautiful creature that had saved his life, had passed away. She that had ingested the toxins and poisons from his wounds had now succumbed to the effects of those substances. Tears rolled down from his huge, sad eyes as he once again picked her up in his mouth and took her back into the wood to her toad colony. When he arrived with her at the colony, he explained everything that had happened. The colony thanked him for bringing her home, saying they would give her a decent burial and elect a new toad queen.

"Big black Bob reared up on his hind legs and placed his two front legs on an ash tree. He opened his mouth and roared, 'I am big black Bob of Bobbits Lane and I declare, in the presence of your toad colony, that I will roam this wood and surrounding area for all time! And if ever a toad queen is in trouble, in danger, or needs help in any way, send for me and I will be there at a gallop to help them if I can!'

"So you see," said the toad queen, "by giving her life for big black Bob, my ancestor left a lasting legacy. Some of the toxins and poisons she had ingested mingled and merged in her stomach and made its way into her polliwogs. But it did not destroy all of them. Seven of them survived; four females and three males survived into their adulthood and bred with various other toads. When their polliwogs were born they had a little more immunity to the toxins, and each generation after them evolved more and more. Then, after many eons, a time came when all newborn polliwogs had complete resistance to the poisons and toxins of their ancestors for the poisons had been dispatched from their insides to their outer dry and warty skin. Ever since that time, toads' glands can produce a poisonous or toxic secretion that helps them to defend themselves from many predators"

"That is a very interesting and moving story," I said, "I will tell that story to many people, children and adults alike. But what has that got to do with you sitting on the back of a horse?"

"Thank you," she said. "Well, two darks ago I set out on my dutiful journey from the wood to the breeding ponds. I had not ventured far when I was attacked and I felt my hind legs being torn from my body. I looked over my shoulder to see a contrary, scheming stoat ready to swallow me, but I squirted him with some of my poison and he ran off in terror. Sadly, he had my hind legs with him. I was unable to move any further, so I just lay there, expecting the worst. When other toads on their way to the ponds spotted me, they reminded me of the vow of big black Bob of Bobbits Lane. Some of them sent for our dear friend and earlier tonight he arrived in the wood and placed me on his back and carried me down here to wait for our other good friends - you lot, the dark lane toad transporters."

We were all silent as we listened to this beautiful creature, then we were sad when she said, "This will be my last journey. As with my ancestral toad queen, I too will not return to the colony after I have spawned. I am ready now; please take me the rest of the way in your bucket and I shall say farewell to the totally true friend of toad queens, big black Bob of Bobbits Lane." She said something in the ear of the big horse, we could not hear what passed between them, all we saw were buckets of tears falling from the huge sad eyes of the big black Bob. I lifted Sally up high; she had a little bucket in her hands.

When Sally reached the toad queen she said lovingly, "Come with us now, toad queen - your bucket awaits." Sally picked the toad queen off the horses back and placed her in the bucket, then I lowered them down to the ground. We all could see the injuries she had sustained, and we also knew it would be her final journey. We walked slowly to the pond's edge, and each one of us in turn said goodbye to the toad queen as Sally lifted her out of the bucket and placed her beside the water. The beautiful toad queen turned her head and looked at all of us. She didn't say anything - she was probably too weak, but we all knew what she wanted to say. She turned and, with her two front legs, she clasped a reed and entered the water. A male toad heard the little splash and made his way to her and climbed on her back, clutching her as all male toad's clutch their females. We watched as the two of them disappeared through a mass of reeds and toad spawn, knowing we would never see that toad queen again. But her descendants will survive and be seen, just as long as there are kind, dedicated human beings like brave Sally to venture out on winter nights with their parents, buckets, torches, high-vis jackets, clipboards, head torches, hand torches, and suitable clothing, saving them from danger. And failing that, there will always be big black Bob of Bobbits Lane to ensure that all future toad queens, if ever in peril, will be escorted safely to their breeding ponds.

The Tump

For many years, wolves and bears roamed Suffolk, but they always seemed to get a bad press. Persecution and habitat loss was their main enemy. Lack of food played its part too, especially with the wolves. And when a new food source comes along, one must grab it with both paws.

Sometime around 300 BCE, brown hares became a common sight in East Anglia. They bred well, and each mother hare could give birth to three or four leverets at a time up to four times a year. So, within a couple of hundred years, the beautiful brown hares became well established as their population grew. But the more of you there are, the more your predators will love you. The long-established native wolves took an instant liking to a new succulent form of sustenance - the brown hares.

For hundreds of years life continued in this way for those

brown hares. Not many leverets could outrun a wolf and therefore many would not live to reach adulthood. So there came a time when the brown hare population was in decline. The adult hares' council gathered at a hares' awareness conference to debate their survival and try to establish a much-needed danger warning system. Many ideas were floated and considered, but no ideal solution was found. That was until a jill leveret that had sneaked into the conference "forms" suggested sound as a means of warning other hares of danger. Some pooh-poohed her idea and some laughed at her. "Whatever do you mean, 'sound'?" laughed one adult buck, "We can't make sounds, we can only squeak!"

"Well," the jill replied, "when I wanted to learn how to box, my mum wouldn't let me. She said boxing was only for bucks. So I got very angry and lost my temper. I then started to jump up and down and stomp on the ground with my big, powerful hind legs. My father came running home and he said, 'Whatever are you doing, our young jill? What is all that noise? I could hear it a half mile away!' So if my father could hear me a half mile away, then most of our colony would be able to hear it, too."

"And your point is?" asked another adult buck.

"My point is this," she said. "If we had a few 'guardians' on lookout while some of us may be working or grazing or sleeping or looking after our young, then at the first sign of danger, the guardians should 'tump' by jumping up and down and stomping on the ground. The sound would travel along the ground for at least a half mile, alerting our nearest neighbours to a danger and giving them time to scarper and hide."

They all looked at the jill with wonder. "Could you please give us a demonstration?" asked an adult jill.

"By all means," said the leveret jill, and proceeded to lead them to an isolated copse. "Now, let us form a few mini groups and then run off in all directions for a half mile. Me and my two friends will stay here and tump. As soon as you hear our tump then you should tump back."

Well, everything went according to plan. The council mini groups ran off for at least half a mile in their favoured directions, and the jill and her two friends jumped, tumped, and stomped. Within seconds they heard the council tumping back! This was a major breakthrough for brown hare security.

The council agreed that the leveret jill's method, the 'tump,' was their best form of defence. They all congratulated her for her brilliant idea, saying that all brown hares owed her a debt of gratitude and that from now on all jill's would be allowed to box if they wanted too. And, of course, many of them did want to box and many of them got very good at it and were well able to box the ears of young bucks that wouldn't take "no" for an answer. During the months of March and April, if you're lucky enough, you can see the wonderful spectacle of jills and bucks as they box in fields, near the woods, or some farmland.

Ever since then, once there was a sniff or a sound of a wolf, or any other danger, the guardian brown hares would jump, tump, and stomp, knowing that the sound would travel along the ground to warn their family, friends and colony of danger.

Working together, looking out for each other, was the best way to survive. More leverets were reaching adulthood than ever before. Then, centuries later, the brown hares noticed creatures similar to them that were appearing in fields and hedgerows close by. They were rabbits that had been introduced for hunting, food, and fur. The hares, at first, didn't realise the "newbies" were their far distant cousins. When they found that the rabbits were not a threat, they invited them to live close by until they got familiar with their new surroundings. Because rabbits burrow to make their homes and warrens, and hares live mostly above ground in "holds," the hares decided they would teach their new neighbours the importance of security and teach them how to tump. As time went by, the Rabbits became experts in the importance and method of tumping and they, too, adopted it as their preferred form of an early warning system.

Between them they created a tump nursery. This was beneath a small hill where rabbits would burrow and construct warrens for the brown hares to come along and teach them how to tump. It took up to three years for each doe and kit to learn, but, once they had learned, all the rabbits and hares in the neighbourhood felt much safer. And tump building continues to this very day. In an area of Suffolk called Ravenswood, not far from Ipswich, the local wildlife group oversaw the completion of a secret tump nursery that was built to house and teach many thousands of jills and bucks and does and kits how to tump. Although you may not see many of these wonderful creatures around, you can be sure they are not far away and ready to jump, tump, and stomp if there is the slightest sign of danger in their environment. So please, keep your ear to the ground, and notify the local rangers if you hear or see any suspicious behaviour in the vicinity of the tump nursery.

The Womist

Strange things can be encountered if you happen to walk in an ancient wood just before sunrise on a cold and frosty February morning.

A few years ago, I was walking through an ancient wood in Ipswich. It was mid-February, about 6.30am, and it was frosty. The reason I was walking in the wood at that time of the morning was "Toad Patrol." I was involved with a local group of toad patrollers that went out in the evenings about ninety minutes before sunset and again in the mornings about ninety minutes before sunrise. We would pick toads off a remote lane to save them from any vehicles using the lane. We would put them in buckets for their own safety, carry them to their breeding ponds, and release them. That is another story for another time (see the story of "The Toad Queen").

On this particular morning, I was alone on patrol. Not many people liked the early morning shift, but I loved that time of day and with my bucket, high-vis jacket, and torch, I was always willing to "rise and shine."

As it was a cold, frosty morning, I knew not many toads would be on the move. I walked up and down the lane a couple of times, but as there was no sign of any amphibians, I decided that I would take a shortcut back to my car through the wood. The faint light of a new day was just appearing above the woodland and, with torch in hand, I entered the ancient wood.

I knew this wood and its paths pretty well because I worked there as a volunteer warden. As I walked along the middle path I saw something very strange in the dim light ahead of me. It seemed to be moving by spinning and swirling slowly and weaving about the trees. At first I thought it was a coil of chicken wire. It was a greyish colour, about one meter high and about twenty centimetres in diameter. I walked slowly and silently a short distance behind the 'coil' and once when I stopped, the 'coil' stopped. Then we both walked a little further and when the 'coil' stopped, I stopped

I was beginning to notice a pattern appearing in its movements. Sometimes it spun, swirled, and veered its way off the path towards fallen trees. It would stop for a few seconds as if it was looking for something. These actions continued for some time until, once again, it spun, swirled slowly, and veered away from the path to another fallen tree. This time was different: this time it made its way to the pit end of the uprooted tree. I noticed that although this tree had been uprooted in a storm, it hadn't fallen to the ground. It had fallen on to a tall ash tree and was being held up at an angle by the ash, with the crown facing the sunrise. The "coil" seemed to roll itself on to the bottom of the tree and lie down. I hid myself behind an oak tree so I could see what was happening without being seen, and what I saw will stay with me forever! From the end of the "coil" at the pit end, changes had begun. Slowly, at first, two shoulders and a neck appeared. Shortly after came a head, with its hair all colours of the rainbow in braidsof dazzling dew, followed by a face with beautiful facial features.

I was astonished at what I was witnessing, for this was the elusive "Womist" - a beautiful half woman, half mist creature that enhances our woodland floors each spring. I was just one of a handful of lucky people to ever witness such magic. As she lay on the tree trunk, I heard a blowing sound. I noticed her mouth was open and she was blowing mist up the tree trunk. The mist swirled its way upwards until it reached the branches and then it dispersed throughout the wood. As this was happening, the coil of mist was getting smaller and smaller. Two arms started to grow from the shoulders of the womist. Her long arms grew, then her wrists grew. I was expecting to see two hands growing, but no, that didn't happen, because, from the ends of her two wrists grew a huge fern leaf! Once the ferns had grown she began to flap her arms, just like a large bird flapping its wings. There was a "Whoosh! Whoosh! Whoosh!" as the womist rose from the tree trunk and began flying through the mist, flapping and flapping. She flew this way and that way and hither and thither between the trees, up and along above the ground she flew with her ferns still flapping.

I began to notice that, as she flew and flapped, the ferns on her wrists were beating the mist downwards to the ground, covering much of the woodland floor. The sun was about to rise by now as the womist flew back to the upturned tree trunk and lay down in the same position. This time I heard an inhaling sound, like a sharp intake of breath, and I watched as the remaining mist was drawn through the trees, down the trunk, and into the mouth of the womist. The coil began to get bigger and bigger as the mist was inhaled.

Once all the remaining mist had been drawn in, the womist's appearance began to change. This time the ferns were first to disappear, then her wrists, arms, and shoulders. Then the neck, beautiful face, head, and hair, and all I could see was a greyish coil on the tree trunk.

A few rays of early sunshine had by now penetrated the woodland. From my vantage point I could see tiny green shoots protruding from the woodland floor and it suddenly dawned on me - I knew then what had happened and what it all meant. I stepped out from behind the oak tree to say thank you to the womist, but she was not there, for she had disappeared into the mists of time …

So, remember ...

While walking in an ancient wood, your eyes
keep open wide for here is where the womist
sometimes tries to hide.

She dashes through the dawning dew with ferns
on her wrists, awakening woodland flora, by
dispersing magic mist.

And when you see a bluebell, a snowdrop, or
primrose, beware, for this is where, the womist's
energy flows.

And if you see the womist on a fallen tree, be
silent, be still, believe, or she will surely flee. She
travels twixt the dark and light, twixt morning
and the night, searching for a fallen tree with its
trunk held upright.

With its crown pointing towards the east, that
tree is what she seeks to dwell upon till night is
gone, till first rays of dawn peeks.

Her eyes are of the bluest blue, her lips are of
cherry hue, her hair is all colours of the rainbow,
in braids of dazzling dew.

Many spirits tease our woodland trees, and ease
them to the fore, but no creature bar a womist
could so enhance a woodland floor.

About the Author

Gerry Donlon aka Bards Aloud, is a Woodbridge based professional Irish storyteller, poet and writer. He is founder and co-host of Storytelling with Bards Aloud (a monthly storytelling gathering in Ipswich) he is co-founder of the East Anglian Storytelling Festival and is founder of Poetree Walks with Bards in the Woods, Suffolk.

He has performed at festivals in England and Ireland, including: The East Anglian Storytelling Festival, Cambridge Folk Festival, Folk East, the Glens Storytelling Festival, Scéalta Beo festival, the Spirit of Beowulf community Festival, Woodbridge Ambient Music Festival and he also performs tales from a hammock at Holywells Park!

He has worked with the National Literacy Trust, Suffolk Councils and the Thomas Wolsey 550. His style of storytelling also takes him to schools, Libraries, carnivals, fetes, parties, Wildlife events etc. His stories have been described as "stories comic and stories quirky"

Acknowledgements

With huge thanks to Softwood Books and their friendly staff for their work and advice, and for supporting me on Anthology 1. To Kelly Will for her front cover and interior illustrations, and Holly Green for coming to my rescue and helping by typing up a few of my stories.

www.ingramcontent.com/pod-product-compliance
Lightning Source LLC
Chambersburg PA
CBHW012237190626
46810CB00021B/3443

* 9 7 8 1 0 6 8 2 5 9 6 0 9 *